GOGGLES™

THE BEAR WHO DREAMED OF FLYING

BOOK 1

WRITTEN BY JONATHAN GUNSON

ILLUSTRATIONS BY RICHARD ROBINSON
& JONATHAN GUNSON

There once was a very small bear who dreamed of flying.

Everyone told him he was too little to fly.

But he always wore flying goggles, just in case they changed their minds, which is why all his family called him 'Goggles'.

$\mathcal{H}$e dreamed about flying at breakfast.
He dreamed about flying when tucked up in bed.
He even dreamed about flying in the bath!

And he always took a jar of honey with him,
because all that flying can make a bear hungry.

But even though Goggles was a very small bear, he knew a very big secret.

His grandparents, Growlville and Wilma Wright, had built an airplane.

They called it 'The Wright Flyer'.

They wanted to be the first bears to fly, but couldn't find an airplane fuel that would work.

On the first try, it crunched into a tree.
On the second try, it crashed into a haystack.
On the third try, it ran into a pond ...

SPLOOSH!

*I*f only they could find the right flying fuel.

They tried lemonade, but it was too fizzy.

They tried custard, but it was too gluggy.

And ketchup was too slurpy, and chocolate too gooey.

Then one day, Goggles had a great idea for fuel.

He whispered it to Grandpa.

Can you guess what it was?

Cheese?

At last the plane would fly.

The great day arrived for the first flight of the honey-powered Wright Flyer.

Take-off was at sunrise and a big crowd was invited to watch.

oggles wanted to fly too, but
everyone said it was too dangerous.
So, while no-one was looking, he sneaked
into the back of the airplane.

... Shsssh!

Grandpa Growlville started the engine.
The propeller whizzed and whirred.

The Wright Flyer began to move, faster and faster,
and then ...

The plane soared into the bright blue sky.

... ZOOOM!

$\mathcal{H}$igher and higher it flew.

Soon they were sailing around the clouds.

It was soooo beautiful!

But then ...

Disaster!

The Wright Flyer ran out of honey and began to
fall from the sky. "If only we had more fuel!"
cried Grandma Wilma.

*S*uddenly, Goggles popped up from
his hiding place.
"EMERGENCY HONEY!"
he shouted.

Grandma had no time to be
shocked to see him.

The engine spluttered,
then roared back to life
... VOOOM!

She quickly poured the honey
into the fuel tank.

The airplane flew safely back to the Bearfield
and landed in front of the cheering crowd.

Grandpa announced that Goggles had saved the day!
The crowd cheered even more loudly.

But Goggles just smiled and waved. He was happy his
grandparents were safe, and what's more, he was one of
the Wright Bears, the first bears to fly.

The Wright Brothers, First Humans To Fly

Before the Wright Brothers, flying seemed like an impossible dream. But the brothers were determined to succeed, and built a plane they called the 'Wright Flyer'.

Orville Wright Wilbur Wright

At first, it failed to fly.
But they kept trying, and on
17 December 1903, at Kitty Hawk,
North Carolina, it flew for the very first time.

This book was inspired by their courage, determination and their amazing achievement.